REINDEER

ROE DEER

WOOD
MOUSE

WOLVERINE

WILD BOAR

AUK

The author and publisher would like to thank Alison Roberts
of the Ashmolean Museum, Oxford, for her invaluable help in the making of this book.

First U.S. edition 2007

Library of Congress Cataloging-in-Publication Data is available.

Library of Congress Catalog Card Number pending

ISBN 978-0-7636-3474-2

2 4 6 8 10 9 7 5 3 1

Printed in Singapore

This book was typeset in Century Old Style.
The illustrations were done in ink and watercolor.

Candlewick Press
2067 Massachusetts Avenue
Cambridge, Massachusetts 02140

visit us at www.candlewick.com

CANDLEWICK PRESS
CAMBRIDGE, MASSACHUSETTS

STONE AGE BOY

SATOSHI KITAMURA

An amazing thing happened to me one day.
I was wandering in the woods
when I tripped and found myself
falling down,

down,

down.

When I woke up, I was in a cold, dark place.

I could see daylight in the distance, and I stumbled toward it.

Outside, everything was different.

I realized I was lost—completely lost.

So I walked and walked

and walked. . . .

Then, to my relief, I saw someone—a girl.

She was about my age, but she didn't look like any of the girls I knew.

And I don't think I looked like any of the boys she knew.

She took me home to meet her family—and what a family it was!

They looked very strange, but they were nice to me and gave me some stew.

I couldn't understand anything they were saying,

but I figured out that my new friend's name was Om.

Then I must have fallen asleep.

The next morning, Om showed me around the camp.

Everyone seemed busy and had a job to do.

Over the next few days, I saw so many things I'd never seen before.

Om's people had no knives or forks, no plastic—not even any metal.

Everything was made of wood, stone, or animal skins.

MAKING FIRE

Om's people made fire by striking stones together or by spinning a wooden drill. They used fire for cooking, to keep warm, and sometimes to scare animals.

MAKING TOOLS

They made tools by a process I later learned is called flint knapping.

The flints are chipped, trimmed, and sharpened, and then made into knives, spearheads, and scrapers for cleaning animal skins.

I gave it a try, but it was very difficult.

USING TOOLS

Om's family used tools to make wood, antlers, and bones into bowls, spears, and ornaments.

Cut a slice out of a bone . . .

sharpen it on a grindstone . . .

pierce a hole.

It's a sewing needle!

Ornaments

16

They used a throwing stick to make their spears go faster and farther.

PREPARING & USING ANIMAL SKINS

scraping the hide clean . . .

cutting it . . .

drying it . . .

piercing holes . . .

and sewing it together.

Om's family made clothing by skinning a deer . . .

PREPARING & COOKING FOOD

Om's family had many ways of preparing food:

cutting meat

drying meat

drying fish

smoking meat

boiling soup by putting a red-hot stone into a leather bag

grilling meat

One afternoon we went to the river.

The little kids picked berries and nuts, but Om and I watched the men fishing.

They held their pointed spears high and stood as still as trees.

Suddenly—*swoosh!*—their spears dropped like lightning,

then came up again, spiking wriggling silver fish.

Suddenly a boy ran up, shouting and pointing to the hills. At once, several people grabbed their spears and followed him. Om and I followed them.

Slowly, slowly, we crept forward until we saw—a reindeer!
It was standing alone, munching the grass.

At a signal, the others ran toward it, yelling and throwing their spears.

Om and I didn't have spears, but we yelled anyway. It was so exciting!

A spear caught the reindeer in its side, and it fell to the ground.

That night, we had a party to celebrate.

We cooked the reindeer over a great fire, and there was music and dancing.

I joined in on air guitar.

As the days became weeks, Om and her people

taught me many things. I was very happy.

Then onc day, Om took me to a special place.

We walked a long way until we came to the mouth of a cave.

Om struck flint stones together to make fire. She lit a torch and we went in.

Wow!

It took me a moment to realize that the animals were only paintings.

In the flickering light of the torch, they looked real,

as if they were running all around us.

Om went over to the tools and paint the artists had left and began to draw.

Suddenly, I saw something move in the darkness.

It was a bear—a big, furious cave bear!

I shouted at Om to run

and turned to face the bear with my spear.

I felt very small.

Suddenly the ground gave way . . .

and I found myself

falling down,

down,

down.

When I woke up, the bear was gone.

So was Om.

I rushed outside.

The air felt . . . different. Warmer.

I walked a long way, calling for Om. But I never found her.

Instead, I found I was back home.

When I told my family what had happened, they didn't believe me.

They said I'd only been gone a few hours

and I must have fallen asleep and dreamed it.

Years passed, but I never forgot my friend Om.

I am an archaeologist now (that's me in the glasses).

Everywhere I go, I look in the past for signs of Om.

And I never stop learning from her and her people.

Was it a dream? Maybe . . .

maybe not.

Index

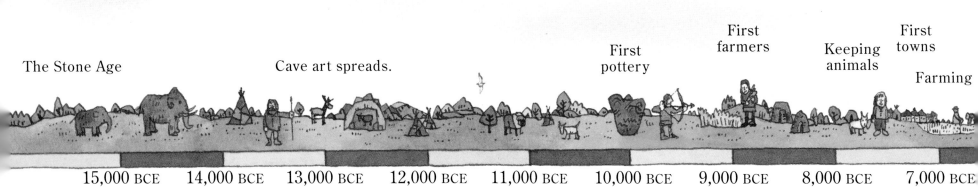

First pottery

First farmers

Keeping animals

First towns

The Stone Age   Cave art spreads.   Farming

15,000 BCE   14,000 BCE   13,000 BCE   12,000 BCE   11,000 BCE   10,000 BCE   9,000 BCE   8,000 BCE   7,000 BCE

Author's Note

I've always been interested in cave paintings. I'd seen them in photos and books for years, and they fascinated me. So one summer I decided to go to the south of France, where many of the caves are, and see them for myself. It was one of the most memorable experiences of my life. They were painted so beautifully—whoever did them must have drawn a great deal, and the animals must have been very important to them. But what struck me above all was the sheer joy in the work. I could see that the artists were having a great time—the animals looked as though they were running and dancing around in the dark caves. This book is the result of my daydreams about those painters and all the people of the Stone Age.

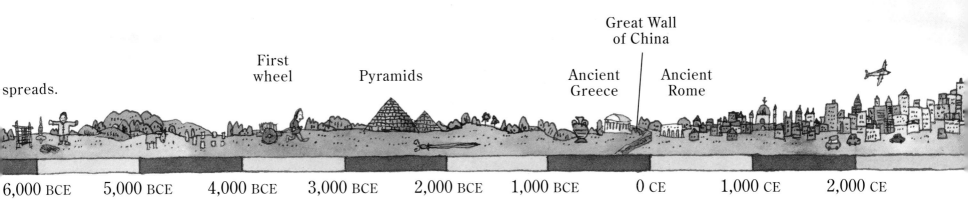

spreads.

First wheel

Pyramids

Ancient Greece

Great Wall of China

Ancient Rome

| 6,000 BCE | 5,000 BCE | 4,000 BCE | 3,000 BCE | 2,000 BCE | 1,000 BCE | 0 CE | 1,000 CE | 2,000 CE |

WOOLLY RHINOCEROS

ARCTIC FOX

RED DEER

PINE MARTEN

DISCARD

MOUNTAIN HARE